Bb

is for bouncing ball!

When I throw my big shiny ball it bounces
away from me ... bounce, bounce, bounce.

Cc  is for cat

Our cat is called Ginger. No cat is as nice
as she is.

MY FIRST
ABC

Shirley Hughes

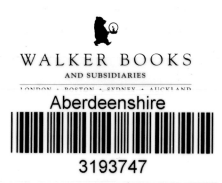

WALKER BOOKS
AND SUBSIDIARIES
LONDON • BOSTON • SYDNEY • AUCKLAND

Aa is for aeroplane

High in the sky, an aeroplane zooms by.
Olly and I wonder how far away it is going.

Dd

is for Dad who is very
good at cooking ...

and for our dog,
Buster, who always
wants to join in
with everything
we are doing.

Ee is for everyone

This is my family: Mum, Dad, Olly and me.

Ff is for farm animals

There is a place in the park where we go and see them up close.

Gg is for Grandma and Grandpa

They are very special. They often come to visit and look after us sometimes when Mum and Dad are busy.

Hh  is for hats

We have some great hats in our dressing up box.
Olly likes to try them on, even if they are too big
for him.

Ii  is for ice cream

Grandpa always treats me to an ice cream
when we go to the park together.

Jj 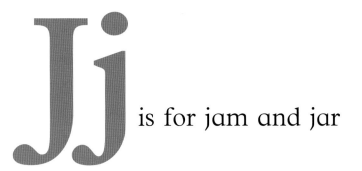 is for jam and jar

When we've finished a jar of jam we can use
it for water to wash our paintbrushes and
keep our colours clean.

Kk is for Katie – that's me!

And this is my little brother Olly.

Ll is for leaves

In the autumn they turn all kinds of beautiful colours and you can wade through them when they fall from the trees.

Mm is for Mum

I love having a cuddle with
Mum at the end of the day
when she reads my
bedtime story.

Nn is for noise

Olly and I can make lots of noise, especially when I am dancing and singing and he joins in with a saucepan and spoon.

Oo is for Olly, of course!

He can be annoying sometimes, but he loves it
when we spend time together and we play some
great games.

Pp is for play-group

I have lots of fun at play-group with my friends, jumping up and down on the big cushions.

Qq is for queen

At Christmas, I got a crown in my cracker and pretended to be a queen.

 is for rainbow

Sometimes, when it's sunny and rainy
at the same time, you can see a beautiful
arc of colours in the sky.

 **S s** is for stories

Olly and I love going to the library on Saturday
afternoons to listen to stories.

Tt is for toys

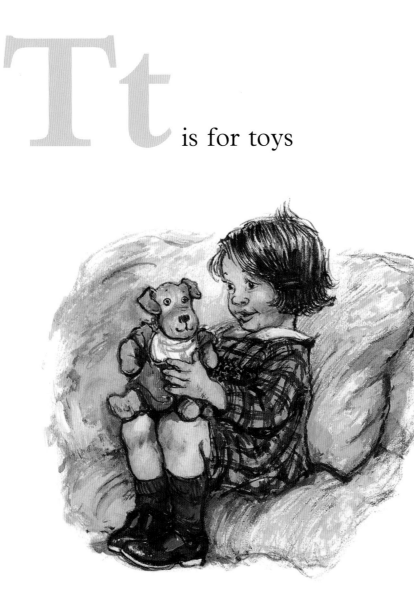

My favourite toy is called Bemily.
She is not quite a hippo and not quite a bear
and I take her with me wherever I go.

Uu is for umbrella

Olly and I have found a really good place to hide.

 is for vacuum cleaner

It vroom-vroom-vrooms when Dad cleans the carpet.

Ww is for wellies

Olly and I need our wellies when we go out and splash in puddles.

Xx is for kisses

Mum gave me an extra-special kiss when I gave her a birthday present all wrapped up in pretty paper.

Yy is for yellow

Yellow is the colour of sunshine, and custard,
and my favourite summery dress.

Zz is for zzzzz

Now it's sleepytime.

Good night, everyone!

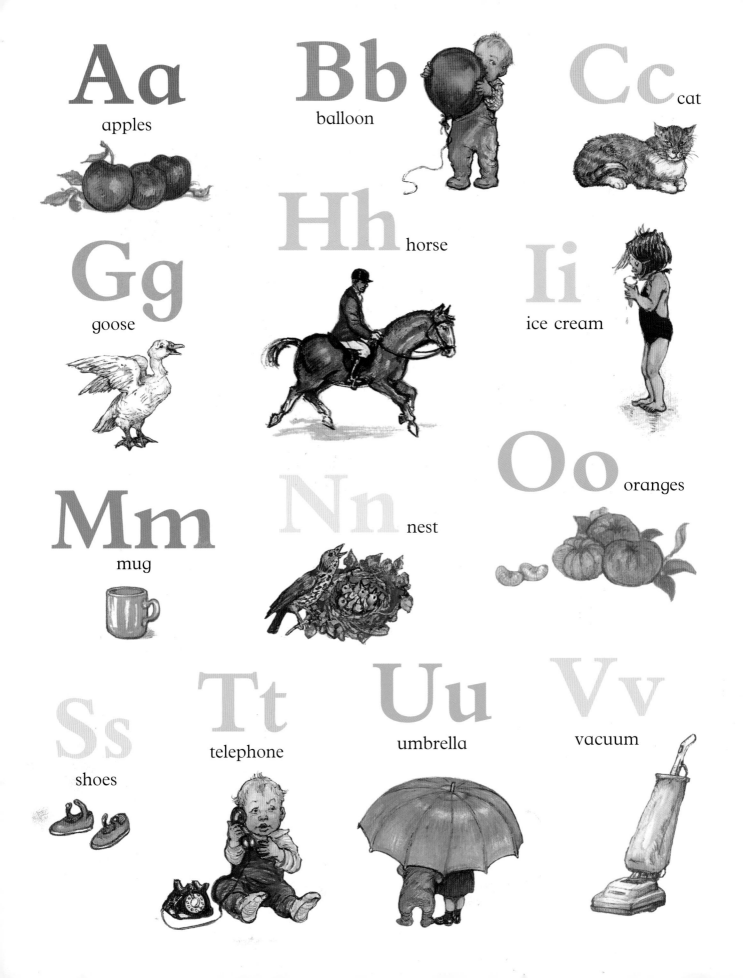

Aa
apples

Bb
balloon

Cc
cat

Gg
goose

Hh
horse

Ii
ice cream

Mm
mug

Nn
nest

Oo
oranges

Ss
shoes

Tt
telephone

Uu
umbrella

Vv
vacuum

The Story of Winter
A Snowflake Falls

Rosie McCormick

HODDER
Wayland

an imprint of Hodder Children's Books

J508·2

Text copyright © Rosie McCormick 2005

Editor: Kirsty Hamilton
Design: Proof Books

Published in Great Britain in 2005
by Hodder Wayland, an imprint of
Hodder Children's Books

The publishers would like to thank the following for allowing us to
reproduce their pictures in this book: Corbis: Niall Benvie title page, 6;
Ariel Skelley 3; George McCarthy 4; Nick Hawkes, Ecoscene 5; Jim
Zuckerman 8; Richard Hutchings 9; Ariel Skelley 11; Michael de
Young 12; Ludovic Maisant 13; Alan Schein Photography Inc 14;
Reuters 15; Steve Terrill 16; Malcom Kitto, Paphilio 17; Steve Austin,
Paphilio 18; Michael S. Yamashita 19; Richard T. Nowitz 20; 21; Jan
Butchofsky-Houser 22; Kennan Ward 23 / Getty Images: Jane Gifford,
Stone 7.

British Library Cataloguing in Publication Data
McCormick, Rosie
A Snowflake Falls: the story of winter. – (The story of the seasons)
1.Winter – Juvenile literature
I. Title
508.2

ISBN 0 7502 4626 X

Printed in China

Hodder Children's Books
A division of Hodder Headline Limited
338 Euston Road, London NW1 3BH

Contents

The sleeping earth

During winter, much of the land is frozen and seemingly lifeless. Many trees are bare and plants stop growing. Instead they rest, preserving their energy. And there are fewer animals about. Some have travelled to warmer places while others are hibernating or sleeping in burrows and dens, protected from the winter chill. All around there is a bleakness that lasts until the first signs of spring.

4

5

Look out, Jack Frost is about!

During the wintertime there is less daylight, or sunshine. And so the days are colder and darker. But even in winter nature can transform a damp, dull landscape – as if by magic.

Sometimes, when you wake up on a winter's morning, you will see the ground, hedges, trees, and even windows covered in a glistening veil of frost. Frost is tiny water droplets that have frozen and been transformed into sparkling crystals of ice.

7

The first snowfall

As the winter temperatures drop, and the days become colder and darker, frozen water droplets, in the form of snowflakes, begin to fall from the sky. If it's cold enough, a thick layer of snow will cover the earth like a soft, white blanket.

Snowflakes are little water droplets and tiny pieces of dust that come together and freeze to create delicate, shimmering plates, stars or prisms – all with six sides.

9

Fun in the snow

A heavy snowfall brings with it some of the most memorable days of winter. For deep, powder-soft snow means endless hours of fun. There are snow-angels to make and snowmen and snow houses to build. There are mountains and hills to ski or sled down and snowball fights to be had. A shimmering snow-covered landscape is one of nature's gifts. It is so enchanting that people cannot help but be tempted out of their warm, snug homes to tumble and roll in the snow.

10

Frozen wonders

When it's so very cold. Cold enough to take your breath away, water freezes and becomes solid. Incredibly, even rivers, ponds and lakes can turn to thick, solid ice and tumbling waterfalls can freeze and cease to fall. Then, waterways glisten in the pale winter sunlight and dagger-like icicles hang down from the eaves of snow-covered roofs. Transformed, the uninviting landscape shimmers and shines like a frozen wonderland.

Blustering blizzards

In winter, it is not uncommon for powerful winter winds and heavy snow clouds to burst, like a dark spell, upon a calm, snow-covered landscape. When this happens the world outside your window can be a frightening and dangerous place.

Powerful, icy winds that blow at 50 or 60 kilometres per hour, and heavy snow fall, can cause severe blizzard conditions. The gusting winds often cause the snow to drift and form deep piles that endanger the lives of people and animals.

15

The holly and the ivy

Despite nature's winter rest, there is some colour to brighten up the stark landscape. The holly bush, with its ruby-red berries stands boldly in the cold, snow-flecked earth. And hawthorn, ivy, mistletoe and rowan are ancient winter companions.

16

Long ago people looked at the grey, lifeless earth and longed for spring. So they decorated their homes with winter plants like mistletoe, thought to contain lucky or magical ingredients. These would comfort them and remind them that spring would soon arrive.

Footprints in the snow

But the beauty of winter cannot hide the fact that for many creatures it is a desperate time. With little growing in the earth, animals such as foxes, rabbits, mice and birds search for food in the frozen hedgerows, fields and gardens. When the last berries and fruits die, and the puddles and streams turn to ice, animals often go hungry.

18

There are some animals, like squirrels, which prepare a winter food store. While others will eat whatever they can find.

Winter festivities

To cheer themselves through the long winter months, many cultures hold winter festivals. In the 19th Century, people in Quebec, Canada, organised the first winter celebration there. Fires were lit on cold, snowy nights and people held activities like dog-sled races. The tradition continues to this very day. Now added to the festivities is a colourful parade that includes costumed characters from French legends.

And in China, the city of Harbin is sometimes called the 'ice city'. During the winter the power of nature is recognised in the sculptures carved from giant blocks of ice.

21

The story of the long winter

A CANADIAN FOLKTALE

Long ago, when only animals walked upon the earth, there was a long winter. Animals struggled to survive. So the Great Council of Animals sent their fastest and bravest to the upper world in search of heat.

When at last they got there, they found a lake, a tipi and two young bears alone, for Mother Bear had gone off hunting.

Inside the tipi were several bags. One bag held rain, one wind, one fog and the last one held heat. The cunning animals stole the bag that held heat. But as they ran away, Mother Bear, who had returned from hunting, chased them.

She was close on their heels when, just in time, the thieves pushed the bag through the entrance in the sky to the lower world. At once heat burst from the bag. And ever since, spring has followed the cold of winter.

23

Glossary

Berry – a small round juicy fruit without a stone

Blizzard – a heavy snowstorm with strong winds

Droplets – tiny drops of water

Energy – a force that makes things move

Frost – ice which forms on the ground on cold nights

Frozen – when something turns to ice

Ice – frozen water

Landscape – natural scenery

Preserve – to save or to keep something safe

Snow – water that freezes into ice crystals and falls to the ground

Solid – something that is firm and stays the same shape

Index

24